EEK & ACK

THE BIG MISTAKE

written by
BLAKE A. HOENA

illustrations by
STEVE HARPSTER

STONE ARCH BOOKS
a capstone imprint

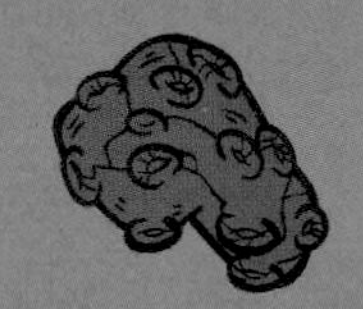

Eek and Ack Early Chapter Books
is published by Stone Arch Books,
A Capstone Imprint
1710 Roe Crest Drive
North Mankato, Minnesota 56003
www.capstonepub.com

Library of Congress Cataloging-in-Publication Data
Hoena, B. A., author.
The big mistake / by Blake A. Hoena ; illustrated by Steve Harpster.
pages cm. -- (Eek and Ack: early chapter books)
Summary: When their sister Bleck dares the boys to conquer Earth, they end up zapping Pluto instead.
ISBN 978-1-4342-6408-4 (hardcover)
ISBN 978-1-4342-6553-1 (paperback)
ISBN 978-1-4342-9234-6 (ebook)
1. Extraterrestrial beings—Juvenile fiction. 2. Brothers and sisters—Juvenile fiction. [1. Extraterrestrial beings—Fiction. 2. Brothers and sisters—Fiction. 3. Science fiction.] I. Harpster, Steve, illustrator. II. Title
PZ7.H67127Bi 2014
813.6—dc23 2013028212

Printed in China by Nordica.
1013/CA21301916
092013 007743NORDS14

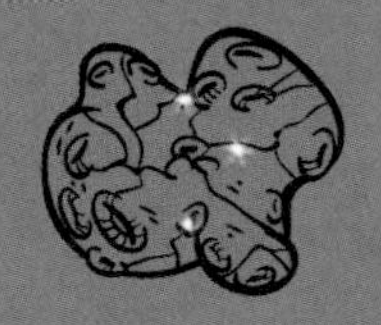

TABLE OF CONTENTS

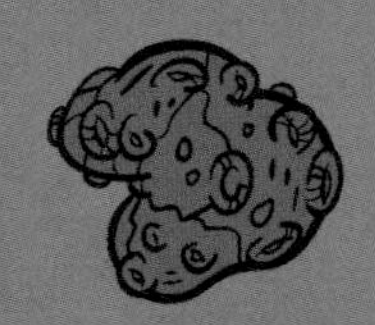

Chapter 1

BLECK'S DARE

One day Eek and Ack were scanning the galaxy. They hoped to find a new planet to conquer.

"Is that one?" Ack asked.

"No, silly," Eek replied. "That's just a UFO."

Suddenly, their big sister Bleck stormed in. "Dad! Mom!" she yelled. "Eek and Ack are playing in the laser room!"

Bleck flashed her brothers an evil smile. "Ha! You're in trouble," she said.

"We haven't done anything," Ack said.

"But we're going to," Eek said. "We're going to conquer a planet."

"In what?" Bleck asked. "That junky spaceship of yours?"

"Once, we flew our junky spaceship all the way to Earth," Ack bragged.

"Ha!" Bleck said. "Earthlings still use flush toilets. Why would you want to go there?"

"Yeah, our vacuum toilets are so much better," Ack said. He looked down at his feet. "It doesn't matter if you miss a little."

"Well, I bet you couldn't even conquer Earth," Bleck said.

Chapter 2

EEK HAS AN IDEA

"Forget about Bleck," said Ack. "Let's go swimming."

"Okay," said Eek. But he was still mad. "First we need to show Bleck we can do what we want to."

"But how can we conquer Earth?" Ack asked. "We don't even have a BB-Blaster. Let's just get to the pool."

Eek ignored him. "Hmm," he thought, staring at his parents' space dome.

Eek looked up at the front window. "I have an idea!" he shouted.

"Oh, no," Ack said. "I get worried whenever you have one of those."

"Remember when we zapped snottle bugs?" Eek asked his brother.

"Yeah, with my magnifying glass," Ack said. "They sizzled and oozed. And they smelled awful, which was awesome!"

"Well, what if we had a giant magnifying glass?" Eek asked.

"Ooh, we could use it to zap earthlings!" Ack shouted.

"Hey," Ack said as he looked up. "Our front window kind of looks like a magnifying glass."

"Exactly!" Eek said with an evil laugh.

The brothers removed the window.

Chapter 3

THAT'S NOT EARTH!

Eek and Ack attached the window to the spaceship. Then they blasted off into space.

The brothers zoomed across the galaxy. They headed to Earth.

When they arrived, Eek parked their spaceship in front of the sun. Earth floated in front of them like a big blue and green marble.

Ack carefully climbed out of the spaceship.

"You aim the magnifying glass," Eek told Ack.

"Which one's Earth again?" Ack asked.

"It's the planet on your left," Eek said.

"Um . . . okay," Ack said. "I hope earthlings stink as much as snottle bugs when they get zapped."

Zap!

"No, Ack! That's not Earth," Eek shouted. "I said your left!"

"Which one's my left?" Ack asked.

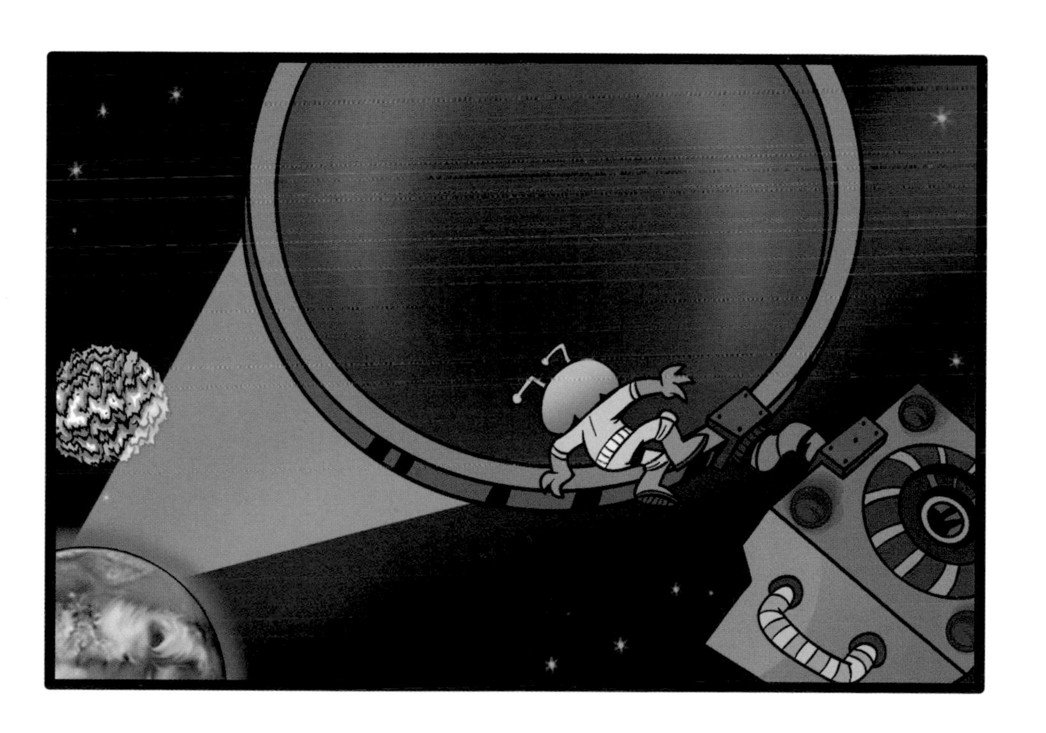

"You always pick your nose with your left hand," Eek said.

"Oh . . ." Ack said. "Hey, did we just zap that frozen planet Pluto?"

"And it looks like we melted it," Eek said. "We better get out of here before someone sees what we did."

Eek and Ack quickly zipped back across the galaxy.

As the boys returned home, Eek said, "Now don't tell Bleck about our big mistake."

"I won't," Ack said. He wiped his head. "Flying near Earth's sun made me so hot."

"Let's go jump in the pool to cool off," Eek said.

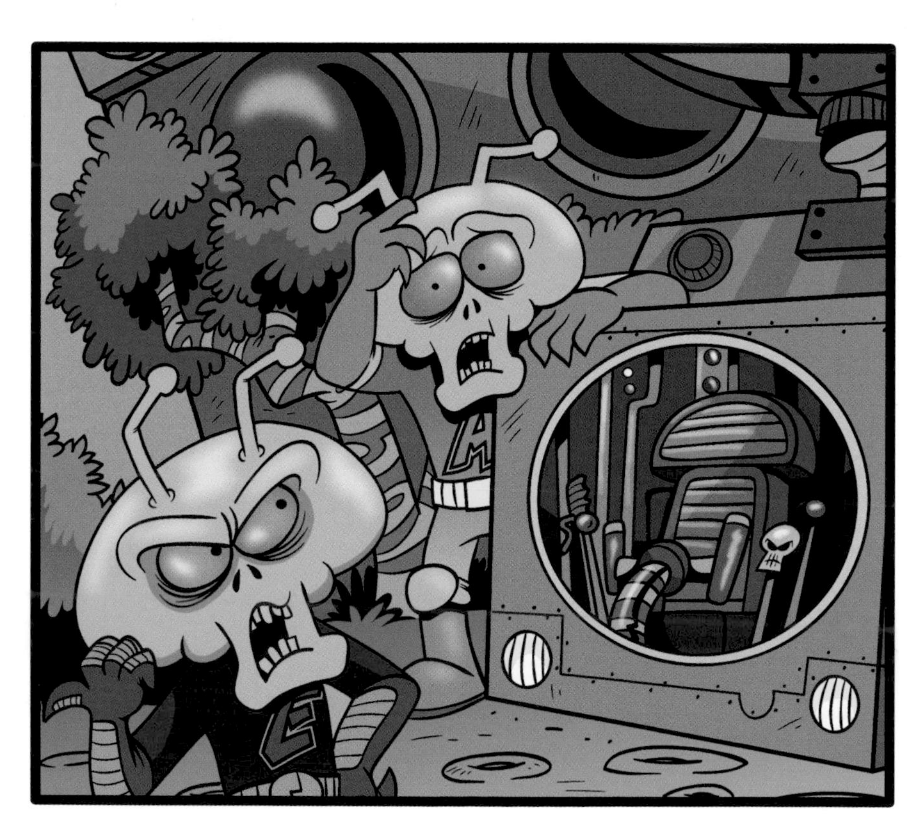

Bleck was sitting by the pool. She was eating a treat.

"What's she eating?" Ack asked.

"I don't know," Eek said. "But it looks so good."

"It's a Pluto-sicle," Bleck said. "They say it came from Pluto."

"Oh, no!" Eek said. "Somebody must have found out about our mistake."

"I don't care," Ack said. "I want a Pluto-sicle, too."

Eek and Ack raced to the Pluto-sicle stand.

At the stand, the owner was telling a story. "There it was," he said. "This ball of ice near Earth. I took it to make my Pluto-sicles. Aren't they tasty?"

"They sure are!" Ack said.

"I'm not sure if this is the ***biggest*** mistake we ever made," Eek said to Ack. "But it has to be the tastiest."

ABOUT THE AUTHOR

Blake A. Hoena once spent a whole weekend just watching his favorite science-fiction movies. Those movies made him wonder why those aliens, with their death rays and hyper-drives, couldn't actually conquer Earth. That's when he created Eek and Ack, who play at conquering Earth like earthling kids play at stopping bad guys. Blake has written more than twenty books for children, and currently lives in Minneapolis, Minnesota.

ABOUT THE ARTIST

Steve Harpster has loved to draw funny cartoons, mean monsters, and goofy gadgets since he was able to pick up a pencil. In first grade, he avoided writing assignments by working on the pictures for stories instead. Steve was able to land a job drawing funny pictures for books, and that's really what he's best at. Steve lives in Columbus, Ohio, with his wonderful wife, Karen, and their sheepdog, Doodle.

GLOSSARY

conquer (KONG-kur)—to defeat and take control of an enemy; Eek always wants to conquer planet Earth.

earthlings (URTH-leen)—creatures from the planet Earth

galaxy (GAL-uhk-see)—a large group of stars and planets

oozed (OOZD)—flowed out slowly

Pluto-sicle (PLOO-toh-si-kuhl)—an ice pop treat made out of ice from Pluto

sizzled (SIZ-uhld)—made a hissing noise

snottle bugs (SNOT-tuhl BUHGZ)—slime-filled bugs found on planet Gloop

tastiest (TAYST-ee-est)—best tasting

vacuum (VAK-yoom)—a machine that sucks up dirt or liquid

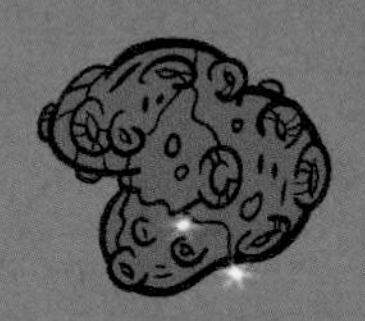

TALK ABOUT THE STORY

1. Why do you think Eek and Ack would like to conquer a planet?
2. Eek and Ack do not get along with their sister, Bleck. Do you ever fight with your siblings?
3. Imagine that Eek and Ack's parents had caught them removing the window from the house. What do you think would happen?

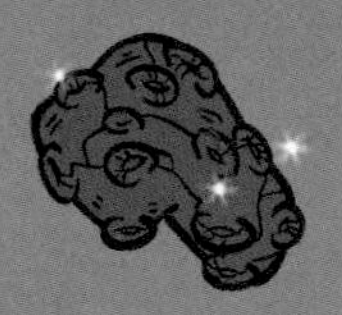

WRITING TIME

1. In this story, Eek and Ack worked together to try to reach a goal. Write about a time when you worked with someone.
2. Create an advertisement for Pluto-sicles. Be sure to tell your customers why Pluto-sicles are so wonderful.
3. Write about your favorite character in this book. Why are they your favorite?

Pluto was once considered the ninth planet in the Milky Way solar system. But in 2006, astronomers reclassified it as a dwarf planet. This is because it shares an orbit with other large objects, such as asteroids. True planets don't share their orbits with other large objects.

Here are some more facts about Pluto the most famous dwarf planet.

- Eek and Ack's giant magnifying glass must have been very powerful to melt Pluto's icy surface. Its average temperature is minus 382 degrees Fahrenheit (minus 230 degrees Celsius).

- One Pluto day equals six Earth days. One Pluto year equals 249 Earth years!
- An eleven-year-old gave Pluto its name. Venetia Burney from Great Britain suggested the name after the Roman god of the underworld.
- Pluto is smaller than the Earth's moon. Its diameter is only half the length of the United States.
- It takes five hours for sunlight to reach Pluto. It takes eight minutes to reach Earth.

THE FUN DOESN'T STOP HERE!

DISCOVER MORE AT...

WWW.CAPSTONEKIDS.COM

FIND COOL WEBSITES AND MORE
BOOKS LIKE THIS ONE AT WWW.FACTHOUND.COM.
JUST TYPE IN THE BOOK ID: 9781434264084
AND YOU'RE READY TO GO!